# Come on, Daisy!

## Jane Simmons

 ORCHARD BOOKS

To my Mum

ORCHARD BOOKS
96 Leonard Street, London EC2A 4RH
*Orchard Books, Australia*
14 Mars Road, Lane Cove, NSW 2066
© Jane Simmons 1998
ISBN 1 86039 541 4 (hardback)
ISBN 1 84121 091 9 (paperback)
First published in Great Britain in 1998
This edition published in 1999
The right of Jane Simmons to be identified as the author and illustrator
of this Work has been asserted by her in accordance with the
Copyright, Designs and Patents Act 1988.
A CIP catalogue record of this book is available
from the British Library
Printed in Singapore

"You must stay close, Daisy,"
said Mamma Duck.
"I'll try," said Daisy.

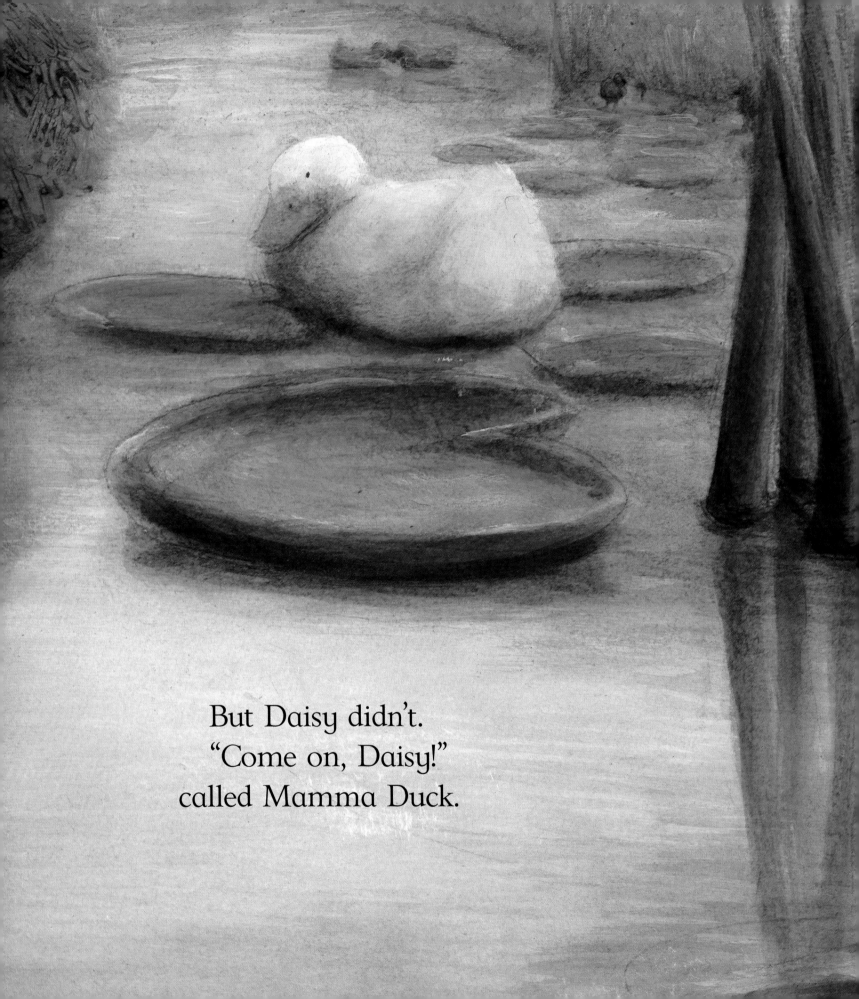

But Daisy didn't.
"Come on, Daisy!"
called Mamma Duck.

But Daisy was watching the fish.

"Come on, Daisy!" shouted
Mamma Duck again.
But Daisy was far away
chasing dragonflies.

"Come here, Daisy!" shouted Mamma Duck.
But Daisy was bouncing on the lily pads.
Bouncy, bouncy, bouncy.
Bong, bong!

"Plop!" went a frog.
"Coo..." said Daisy.
"Gribbit," said the frog.

Bong, plop!

Bong, plop!

Bong, plop!

Splosh!

"Coo!" said Daisy, but the
frog had gone.
"Mamma," called Daisy, but
Mamma Duck had gone.
Daisy was all alone.

Something big stirred underneath her.
Daisy shivered.

She scrambled up on to the riverbank.
Then something screeched in
the sky above!

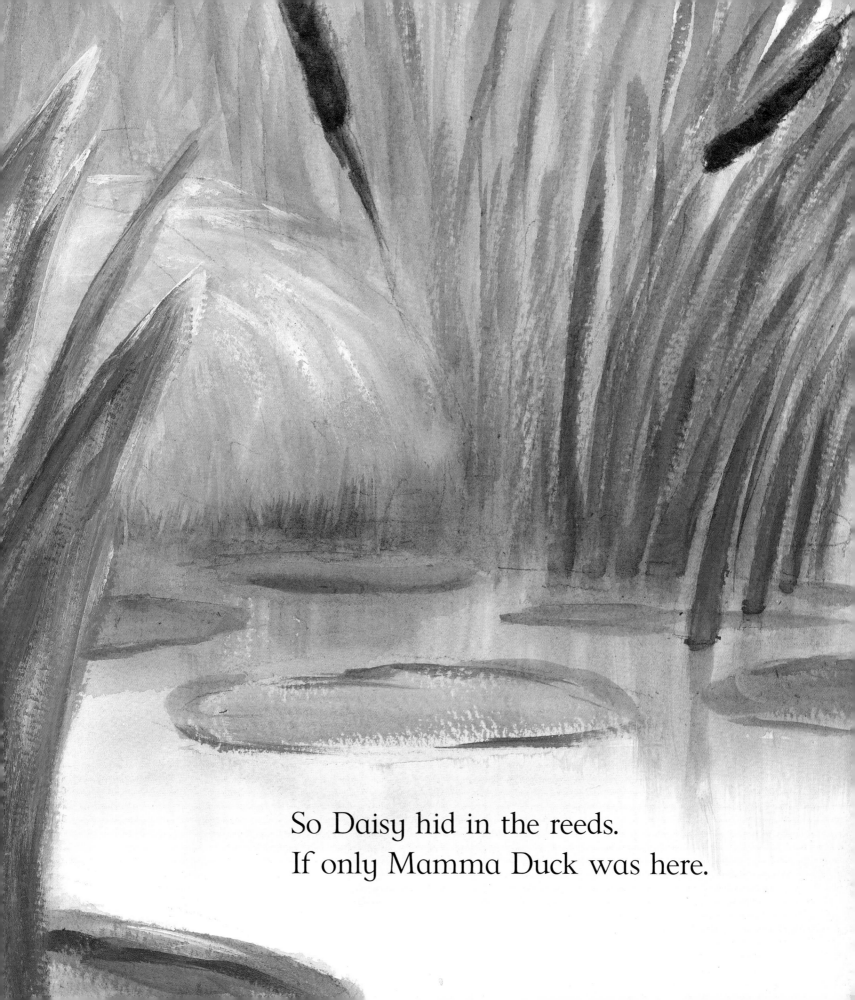

So Daisy hid in the reeds.
If only Mamma Duck was here.

Something was
rustling along the
riverbank.
Daisy could hear
it getting closer...

...and closer,

and closer,

and...

CLOSER...

It was Mamma!
"Daisy, come on!" she said.
And Daisy did.

And even though she played
with the butterflies...

she stayed very close to Mamma Duck.